Dear Parents:

Congratulations! Your child is taking the first steps on an exciting journey. The destination? Independent reading!

STEP INTO READING® will help your child get there. The program offers five steps to reading success. Each step includes fun stories and colorful art or photographs. In addition to original fiction and books with favorite characters, there are Step into Reading Non-Fiction Readers, Phonics Readers and Boxed Sets, Sticker Readers, and Comic Readers—a complete literacy program with something to interest every child.

Learning to Read, Step by Step!

Ready to Read   Preschool–Kindergarten
• big type and easy words • rhyme and rhythm • picture clues
For children who know the alphabet and are eager to begin reading.

Reading with Help   Preschool–Grade 1
• basic vocabulary • short sentences • simple stories
For children who recognize familiar words and sound out new words with help.

Reading on Your Own   Grades 1–3
• engaging characters • easy-to-follow plots • popular topics
For children who are ready to read on their own.

Reading Paragraphs   Grades 2–3
• challenging vocabulary • short paragraphs • exciting stories
For newly independent readers who read simple sentences with confidence.

Ready for Chapters   Grades 2–4
• chapters • longer paragraphs • full-color art
For children who want to take the plunge into chapter books but still like colorful pictures.

STEP INTO READING® is designed to give every child a successful reading experience. The grade levels are only guides; children will progress through the steps at their own speed, developing confidence in their reading.

Remember, a lifetime love of reading starts with a single step!

Visit us on the Web!
StepIntoReading.com
randomhousekids.com

Educators and librarians, for a variety of teaching tools, visit us at RHTeachersLibrarians.com

ISBN 978-0-7364-3596-3 (trade) — ISBN 978-0-7364-8185-4 (lib. bdg.)
ISBN 978-0-7364-3597-0 (ebook)

Printed in the United States of America   10 9 8 7 6 5 4 3 2 1

Disney

Whisker Haven
TALES
with the
palace pets

The Best Ball

adapted by Ruth Homberg

based on the animated short written by Shea Fontana

illustrated by the Disney Storybook Art Team

Random House 🏠 New York

Ms. Featherbon
shows Pumpkin
a letter.

It says Pumpkin
will throw a ball.
Pumpkin loves parties!

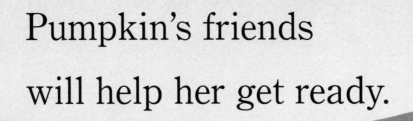

Pumpkin's friends
will help her get ready.

Berry makes cookies.

Oh, no!

Berry eats the cookies!

Treasure gets balloons.

Oh, no!

Treasure floats away!

<u>Pop!</u>

She falls

on a table.

What a mess!

Pumpkin is not ready
to throw a ball.

Pumpkin has an idea.

She adds bows.

She is ready
for the ball!

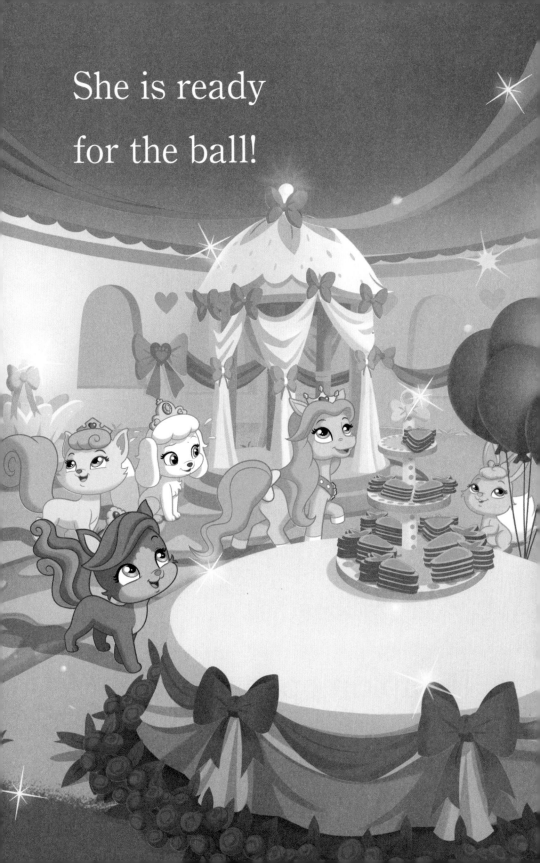

Pumpkin opens the doors.

Where are the guests?

Pumpkin finds them
in the garden
with a ball.

The ball is not a party.

It is a real ball!

Pumpkin will throw it!

Pumpkin gets ready.

Wait!

Petite has an idea.

They will add bows!

Pumpkin's friends
help her.

The ball is ready!

They throw the ball!

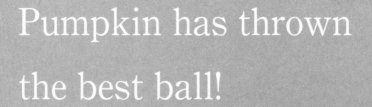

Pumpkin has thrown
the best ball!